Dear Parents:

Congratulations! Your child is taking the first steps on an exciting journey. The destination? Independent reading!

STEP INTO READING® will help your child get there. The program offers five steps to reading success. Each step includes fun stories and colorful art or photographs. In addition to original fiction and books with favorite characters, there are Step into Reading Non-Fiction Readers, Phonics Readers and Boxed Sets, Sticker Readers, and Comic Readers—a complete literacy program with something to interest every child.

Learning to Read, Step by Step!

Ready to Read Preschool–Kindergarten
• big type and easy words • rhyme and rhythm • picture clues
For children who know the alphabet and are eager to begin reading.

Reading with Help Preschool–Grade 1
• basic vocabulary • short sentences • simple stories
For children who recognize familiar words and sound out new words with help.

Reading on Your Own Grades 1–3
• engaging characters • easy-to-follow plots • popular topics
For children who are ready to read on their own.

Reading Paragraphs Grades 2–3
• challenging vocabulary • short paragraphs • exciting stories
For newly independent readers who read simple sentences with confidence.

Ready for Chapters Grades 2–4
• chapters • longer paragraphs • full-color art
For children who want to take t¹
but still like colorful pictures.

STEP INTO READING® is designed to give ⲉ
reading experience. The grade levels are only g   ⱳⲓⱡⱡ progress
through the steps at their own speed, developing   ᵤᵢₔᵤₑₙcₑ in their reading.
The F&P Text Level on the back cover serves as another tool to help you choose the right book for your child.

Remember, a lifetime love of reading starts with a single step!

Text copyright © 1986 by David L. Harrison.
Illustrations copyright © 1986 by Hans Wilhelm, Inc.
All rights reserved. Published in the United States by Random House Children's Books, a division
of Penguin Random House LLC, New York.

Step into Reading, Random House, and the Random House colophon are registered trademarks of
Penguin Random House LLC.

Visit us on the Web!
StepIntoReading.com
randomhousekids.com

Educators and librarians, for a variety of teaching tools, visit us at
RHTeachersLibrarians.com

Library of Congress Cataloging-in-Publication Data
Harrison, David Lee, 1937– .
Wake up, Sun! / by David L. Harrison ; illustrated by Hans Wilhelm.
  p. cm. — (Step into reading. A step 2 book.)
Summary: When Dog wakes up early, in the middle of the night, he launches all the other
farm animals in a worried search for the missing sun.
ISBN 978-0-394-88256-7 (trade) — ISBN 978-0-394-98256-4 (lib. bdg.) —
ISBN 978-0-385-37279-4 (ebook)
[1. Domestic animals—Fiction. 2. Sun—Fiction.]
I. Wilhelm, Hans, 1945– ill. II. Title. III. Series: Step into reading. Step 2 book.
PZ7.H2474 Wak 2003 [E]—dc21 2002013654

Printed in the United States of America 78 77

This book has been officially leveled by using the F&P Text Level Gradient™ Leveling System.

WAKE UP, SUN!

by David L. Harrison

illustrated by Hans Wilhelm

Random House New York

One night,
in the middle of the night,
a flea bit Dog on his ear.
Dog woke up.

"Woof! Woof!" said Dog.
"It must be time
to get up."

Pig woke up too.

"Oink! Oink!" said Pig.

"Be quiet."

"It is time to get up,"
said Dog.

"No, it is not,"
said Pig.
"The sun is not up."

"Where can the sun be?"
asked Dog.

"Maybe it fell in the well,"
said Pig.

Dog and Pig ran to the well.
"Sun! Sun!" said Pig.
"Are you down there?"

Cow woke up.

"Moo! Moo!" said Cow.

"What are you doing?"

"We are looking for the sun,"
said Pig.

"Maybe the sun
is hiding behind the barn,"
said Cow.

Dog, Pig, and Cow
looked behind the barn.
"Come out, Sun!"
shouted Cow.

Chicken woke up.

"Cluck! Cluck!"
said Chicken.

"What is wrong?"

"We can not find the sun,"
said Cow.

Chicken said,
"Maybe the sun
is sleeping late."
"Then we must
wake up the sun,"
said Dog.

All the animals
began to yell.

Cluck! Cluck!

Moo! Moo!

Oink! Oink!

Woof! Woof!

Farmer and his wife
woke up.

"There must be a fox
in the hen house,"
Farmer said.

Farmer ran to the window.

He fired his gun.

BANG! BANG!

The animals stopped yelling.
It was quiet
but not for long.

"WAH! WAH! WAH!"
Farmer's baby woke up
just as the sun
came over the barn.

"Look!" said Dog.
"Farmer's baby
woke the sun!"

From that day on
Dog always played ball
with Farmer's baby.

Pig let her chase him
and pull his tail.

Cow gave her
lots of sweet milk
to drink.

And Chicken laid eggs
for her, one every day.

The animals were very nice
to Farmer's baby.
After all, they knew
she was the only one
who could wake up the sun!